Bialosky's Chr

By Leslie McGuire • Illustrations by Jerry Joyner

A GOLDEN BOOK • NEW YORK
Western Publishing Company, Inc., Racine, Wisconsin 53404

Created by Peggy & Alan Bialosky

Bialosky woke up early. Bialosky always woke up early. He sniffed the air to see what kind of a day it would be.

"I smell Christmas," Bialosky said happily. "Oh, bumblebees! Christmas Eve is tonight!"

"It certainly would be fun," Bialosky thought, "to have a Christmas party and do everything myself.

"Most Christmases someone else finds the tree and decorates the house. Someone else makes Christmas dinner. Someone else wraps the presents.

"This year, I'll do it all myself. Won't my friends be surprised! But I'd better hurry."
He quickly ate his breakfast of honey pancakes and rushed out the door.

"Deck the halls with bears and holly,
Tra la la la la, la la la la.
'Tis the season to be jolly,
Tra la la la la, la la la la!"

Bialosky sang as he trudged through the snow.

"Now all I have to do is find just the right tree," he said.

But finding just the right tree isn't always easy.

He found a nice one, but it was too tall.

He found another nice one, but it was too fat.

Then he found another nice one, but it was too prickly.

Then he found another nice one—and this one wasn't too tall or too fat or too prickly.

But try as he might, he couldn't dig it up. He sat down, feeling very discouraged.

Then he saw a funny little, skinny little tree standing all alone.

"This tree has possibilities," Bialosky thought. He looked at it again. "This tree is looking better and better. In fact, this tree is The One!"

He carefully dug it up and carried it home.

Back home, Bialosky found an old, empty honey pot and he stood the tree up in it. Then he filled the pot with soil to hold the tree up just right.

"Am I forgetting something?" Bialosky said. "Oh, yes, the decorations."

He went into his closet and rummaged
around. Then he dug in his bureau. He
found some spools and some ribbons.
He got some shiny buttons, and some bright
thimbles, and some silver foil. He found
beads, and tissue paper, and little bells.

He cut and he pasted and he threaded
and he sang,
     "We wish you a beary Christmas,
     We wish you a beary Christmas,
     We wish you a beary Christmas
     And a happy new year."

Soon the little tree twinkled and sparkled.

"Am I forgetting something?" Bialosky said. "Oh, yes, the Christmas dinner. I think I'll have something especially Christmasy—like honey. And maybe some honey cakes. And some delicious honey cookies, and sweet potatoes with honey."

Bialosky put on his apron and got to work.

A lot of honey ended up in Bialosky's tummy.

A lot of the cookie batter ended up in Bialosky's tummy, too.

A lot of the honey cake batter ended up on the table (and a little on the walls).

A few of the sweet potatoes got a little burned.

But soon everything was ready.
Bialosky put it all out on pretty plates.
    He hung holly and bows over the door
and the windows. Then he looked around.

"Everything looks great," he said, "but I know I've forgotten something."

"Oh, yes, presents!" Bialosky said. "A tree just doesn't look right without presents underneath."

Bialosky went to his desk and got out his paints and pens and paper. He drew a picture of the view from his window, and a picture of himself, and even a picture of the Christmas tree.

He wrapped the pictures in shiny paper and tied them with ribbons and put them under the tree.

Then he frowned and scratched his ear. "I think I've still forgotten something—but what could it be?"

He was busily thinking, and frowning, and scratching, when there was a loud knock on the door.

"Who could that be?" Bialosky wondered, as he opened the door.

"Merry Christmas,

Bialosky!"

There were all his friends.
"We were so worried about you," Susie
said. "It's Christmas Eve, and we hadn't seen
you all day."
"Now I remember what I forgot,"
Bialosky shouted. "I forgot to invite my
friends! Come right in! I have your presents,
and I have your Christmas dinner all ready.
Aren't you surprised?"

They did come in, and they were surprised, and it was the nicest Christmas party they'd ever had.